P9-CCB-208

Shark Attack!

by ABBY KLEIN

illustrated by
JOHN McKINLEY

Scholastic Inc.
New York Toronto London Auckland
Sydney Mexico City New Delhi Hong Kong

To Jenn,
my best friend and the sister I never had.
Love you tons!

Love,
A.K.

No part of this publication may be reproduced, stored in a retrieval
system, or transmitted in any form or by any means, electronic,
mechanical, photocopying, recording, or otherwise, without written
permission of the publisher. For information regarding permission,
write to Scholastic Inc., Attention: Permissions Department,
557 Broadway, New York, NY 10012.

ISBN 978-0-545-29500-0

Text copyright © 2011 by Abby Klein
Illustrations copyright © 2011 by John McKinley
All rights reserved. Published by Scholastic Inc.
SCHOLASTIC and associated logos are trademarks
and/or registered trademarks of Scholastic Inc.

15 14 13   14 15 16/0

Printed in the U.S.A.   40
First printing, November 2011

CHAPTERS

I have a problem.

A really, really big problem.

My class is going on a field trip
to the aquarium. You can take a
shark quiz at the new shark exhibit,
and if you can answer all the questions,
you win a prize. Everybody says I am
a shark expert, but what if I don't
know all the answers?

Let me tell you about it.

CHAPTER 1

My Lucky Shark's Tooth

Usually my mom has to drag me out of bed. But not today! This morning I woke up even before my alarm clock went off, because I was so excited. My class was going on a field trip to the aquarium. I love the aquarium because it has sharks, and sharks are my favorite things in the whole wide world.

I jumped out of bed and started to get dressed. I put on my hammerhead shark shirt, my shorts that have sharks swimming all over them, my baseball hat that looks like a shark's head, and my shark socks.

"I think I'm all set," I said to myself. "Oh no, I almost forgot . . . my lucky shark's tooth! I can't go to the aquarium without my lucky shark's tooth."

I looked on my nightstand right next to my clock. That's where I always put the tooth right before I go to sleep, but it wasn't there.

I looked on my dresser. It wasn't there, either. Where could it be?

I ran into the bathroom. Since it was so early, my sister, Suzie, wasn't in there hogging it yet.

I threw all the dirty clothes out of the hamper one by one, but I still didn't find it.

Suzie walked into the bathroom. She took one look at me and started to laugh. "Ha, ha, ha, ha, ha!"

"What's so funny?" I asked.

"Your outfit," she said, pointing and laughing.

"What's wrong with my outfit?"

"You look like a dork," said Suzie. "Are you really going to wear all of that shark stuff at one time?"

"Yes, I am, and I'm even missing something."

"What?" asked Suzie. "Shark underwear?"

"Ha-ha, very funny," I said. "No, not shark underwear. I'm missing my lucky shark's tooth. Have you seen it?"

"I'm not sure. Let me think," said Suzie.

"Well, could you think fast?" I asked.

"What's it worth to you?" Suzie said, holding up her pinkie for a pinkie swear.

"Anything," I said. "My class is going to the aquarium today, and I can't go without my lucky shark's tooth."

"Okay, then how about you do my chores for a week?"

"A week? Are you crazy?"

"You said 'anything,'" said Suzie, shoving her pinkie in my face. "Do we have a deal or not?"

I didn't really have a choice. I couldn't go without my lucky shark's tooth, and time was running out. "Fine. Deal," I said as we locked pinkies. "Now, where is it?"

"I think I saw it on the desk in the kitchen," said Suzie.

"You *think*? I thought you knew for sure."

I raced downstairs to the kitchen.

"What's the rush?" asked my mom. "You're usually not even out of bed by now."

"I'm trying to find my lucky shark's tooth. Suzie said she thinks it's on your desk."

My mom walked over to her desk. "Yes, honey, it's right here. I almost vacuumed it up yesterday by accident because it was lying on the floor."

"That would have been a disaster! Good thing you saw it, Mom."

"It must have fallen off your pants. Make sure you put it on tightly today. You wouldn't want to lose it at the aquarium."

"That's for sure. It's my good-luck charm," I said, hooking it on the belt loop of my shorts.

"Now come sit down and have some breakfast. You need energy for your big day. I made your favorite—pancakes."

"Yum," I said, patting my stomach.

My mom put a pancake down in front of me and went back to the stove to make more for Suzie.

I cut the pancake in half. I left one half alone, and I cut the other half into strips. I was moving all the pieces around on my plate when Suzie came into the kitchen.

"Mom! Freddy is playing with his food!" she said.

I glared at her.

My mom came running over. "Freddy, what are you doing? How many times have I told you not to play with your food?"

"But I'm trying to make something, Mom," I said.

"Your food is not an art project."

"But this is going to be really cool, Mom. Watch."

I finished putting the pieces into place. "Ta-da!" I said.

"What is it?" asked Suzie.

"A jellyfish."

"A what?"

"A jellyfish," I said. "This half is the body, and these strips are the tentacles."

"Very clever," said my mom.

I smiled at Suzie.

"Now eat up. You don't want to miss your bus. It's your big day."

"Oh, that's right. It's almost time for the aquarium adventure," my dad said as he walked into the kitchen.

"I know," I said, shoving pancake into my mouth. "I can't wait!"

"Hey, Shark Boy, no seafood," said Suzie. "I don't want to *see* the *food* in your mouth."

"Freddy, little bites, please," said my mom. "Not shark bites."

"I hear they have a new shark exhibit," my dad said.

"Yeah. Robbie and I looked it up on the computer. It's so cool."

"I can't wait to hear all about it," said my mom.

"Maybe we'll even see some pups," I said.

"Puppies?" Suzie said, laughing. "For your information, Ding-Dong, dogs are not sea creatures. I don't think you'll see any puppies today."

"For *your* information, baby sharks are called pups."

"Oh," Suzie mumbled.

"I didn't know that," said my mom. "Finish

up, my little pup. The bus will be here any minute."

I gulped down my orange juice, grabbed my shark backpack, and kissed my parents good-bye.

"Have an awesome time!" said my dad.

"Oh, I will," I said as I pretended to swim toward the front door. "This is going to be the best day ever!"

CHAPTER 2

The Little Mermaid

As soon as we all got to school, our teacher, Mrs. Wushy, said, "We have to get on the bus for our field trip to the aquarium right now. The aquarium is about an hour away, and we want to spend the whole day there since there is so much to see."

"Cool," said Max. "We don't have to learn anything today."

"Oh, you will be learning a lot," Mrs. Wushy said, smiling. "Just not in the classroom."

We all piled onto the bus. My best friend, Robbie, sat down next to me. Of course, Max, the biggest bully in the whole first grade, sat down right in front of us.

"Why does he always have to sit near us?" I whispered to Robbie.

"I don't know," said Robbie. "Don't worry about it. Let's talk about the trip. What are you excited to see?"

"I can't wait to see a mermaid," said Chloe.

Max turned around in his seat. "What did you say?"

"I said I can't wait to see a mermaid."

Max burst out laughing. "HA, HA, HA, HA, HA, HA, HA!"

"Stop laughing at me," said Chloe. "What's so funny?"

"Mermaids are not real," said Max.

"Yes, they are!" said Chloe with her hands on her hips.

"No, they're not," said Max, still snickering.

"The Little Mermaid is real, and she has beautiful red hair just like mine," said Chloe, tossing her fiery red curls in Max's direction.

My friend Jessie was sitting in the seat across from me. She leaned over and whispered, "Does she really think she's a princess?"

We both started giggling.

"Well, Prissy Princess, you're wrong!" shouted Max.

Just then Mrs. Wushy came over to us. "What is going on back here? Max, you may not shout on the bus."

"If you don't believe me, then ask Mrs. Wushy," Chloe said.

"Ask me what?" said Mrs. Wushy.

"About mermaids," said Chloe. "Mermaids are real, right?"

"There are many stories about mermaids, Chloe," said Mrs. Wushy. "But there are no pictures of real mermaids swimming around in the ocean."

"You mean we're not going to see any mermaids at the aquarium today?"

"No," said Mrs. Wushy. "I'm sorry."

Chloe crossed her arms, stuck out her lower lip, and started to pout.

"I have to go back to my seat now, but you all need to keep it down back here," said Mrs. Wushy. "I don't want to hear any more shouting." She looked at Max. "Do you understand?"

Max nodded.

She turned to Chloe. "Understand?"

Chloe nodded and stuck her lower lip out even farther.

"Good," said Mrs. Wushy, and she went back to the front of the bus.

"I really wanted to see a mermaid," Chloe whined. "My nana even bought me this new camera to take pictures today, and now I won't have anything to take pictures of."

"Why don't you take pictures of the sharks?" said Max, opening and closing his arms like a big shark's mouth.

"Oh no!" said Chloe. "Sharks aren't pretty. Sharks are mean and scary! I don't even want to see them," she said, pretending to shiver.

"Freddy, I bet you can't wait to see the sharks," said Jessie.

I smiled a big smile. "Sharks are my favorite things in the whole wide world!"

"Duh. I think everybody knows that, Shark Breath," said Max, laughing. "All they have to do is look at what you're wearing."

"I like what you're wearing," said Jessie.

"I think it looks lame," said Max.

"I think it looks cool," said Jessie. "Where did you get all that shark stuff?"

"All different places," I said. "You know I love to collect anything that has to do with sharks. My favorite thing is this shark's tooth." I unhooked the tooth from my belt loop and held it up for everyone to see.

"That's cool," said Max.

"I thought you said his shark stuff was lame," said Jessie.

"Well, *that's* cool," said Max.

"I take it with me wherever I go," I said. "It brings me good luck."

"Let me see it," said Max, grabbing at it.

I pulled my hand back. "No. I promised my mom I would take really good care of it today," I said, hooking it back on my pants.

"Where did you get it?" asked Jessie.

"My papa and grammy got it for me at this huge aquarium in New York City."

"Lucky," said Max.

"You know," said Robbie, "there is a new shark exhibit at the aquarium. Freddy and I looked it up on the computer."

"Really?" said Jessie.

"And guess what," I said. "They have real shark eggs."

"Shark eggs. Ha, ha, ha. That's so funny," Max said, butting in. "I thought you were a shark expert. Then you should know that sharks don't lay eggs. Everybody knows that."

Max jumped out of his seat. "Guess what, everybody?" he shouted. "Freddy thinks that sharks lay eggs!"

The whole bus started laughing.

My cheeks got hot.

"Max," said Mrs. Wushy, "what did I say about shouting on the bus? You need to come sit with me. And Freddy is right. Some sharks do lay eggs."

Now Max turned bright red.

"What do shark eggs look like?" asked Jessie.

"They aren't oval-shaped, like chicken eggs," I said. "They are kind of long and flat."

"Wow! I can't wait to see one," said Jessie.

"Me either," I said. "I don't think I can wait much longer."

"I don't think you'll have to," said Robbie. "It looks like we're here!"

CHAPTER 3

Fish, Fish, and More Fish!

When the bus pulled up in front of the aquarium, we all got off.

"Come with me," said Mrs. Wushy, "and please stay together." We followed her inside.

"Good morning, everyone," said our guide. "My name is Jon, and I'll be showing you around today. If you have any questions, please don't be afraid to ask. I love to answer questions."

Chloe's hand shot up.

"Great! My first question of the day," said Jon.

"Oh no," Robbie whispered to me. "Here we go again."

"Do you have any mermaids here?" Chloe asked.

"Is she for real?" whispered Jessie.

"No, I'm sorry. We don't have any mermaids, but we do have some really beautiful creatures. If you just come this way, I'll show you some of my favorites."

We followed Jon into the first room. There were a bunch of tanks with all kinds of sea creatures.

"Oooooh, look!" said Chloe. "Sea horses." We all ran over to see them. "Mermaids ride on sea horses."

"Mermaids, mermaids, mermaids," said Max. "Is that all you can talk about, you pink, fluffy poodle?"

"Mrs. Wushy! Mrs. Wushy!" Chloe yelled. "Max called me a dog."

"I did not," said Max.

"Yes, you did," said Chloe. "You called me a poodle."

I giggled.

"Max, you may not call Chloe names."

"But she is annoying me. She keeps talking about mermaids!"

"Just because she is annoying you, it doesn't mean that you can call her names. And, Chloe, you need to stop arguing with Max. Do you understand?"

They both nodded.

"Good, then let's listen to what Jon has to say."

"Sea horses are very interesting," said Jon.

"They're so tiny," said Jessie.

"Some sea horses can be as small as one inch. They are not very good swimmers, so it's hard for them to protect themselves in the ocean," said Jon.

"What do they do to stay safe?" I asked.

"They like to hide in coral or sea grass," said Jon. "And they can change their color to match what's around them. Does anyone know what that is called?"

"Camouflage!" said Robbie.

"Very good!" said Jon. "It *is* camouflage. They can turn bright colors if they are hiding in coral, or they can turn brown or gray if they are in sea grass. When they change color, it makes it hard for predators to see them."

"Hey, that one looks like it has its tail wrapped around the coral," I said.

"It does," said Jon. "Sea horses wrap their tails around a piece of coral or sea grass so they don't float away from their hiding place."

"Kind of like how a monkey wraps its tail around a tree branch," said Robbie.

"Exactly," said Jon. "Do you see how he has a snout at the end of his long nose?"

"Yes," we all said.

"He sucks up food with that snout," Jon said.

"So his snout is like a vacuum cleaner," Jessie said, giggling.

"Yes. The sea horse sucks up tiny shrimp and plankton with its snout. Since they can't really swim, they just wait for their food to float by."

"It would be fun to be at the beach and have a hamburger or a piece of pizza float by you," I said, laughing.

"Do you want me to tell you something about sea horses that most people don't know?" said Jon.

"Tell us! Tell us!" we shouted.

"The male sea horse has a little pouch," said Jon.

"Like a kangaroo!" said Chloe.

"The female sea horse lays her eggs in his pouch. The male sea horse takes care of the eggs for two months."

"You mean the mom doesn't sit on the eggs or take care of them, like a hen does?" asked Jessie.

"Nope," said Jon. "The dad carries the eggs in his pouch and protects them. When the eggs hatch, the baby sea horses swim out of the pouch."

"Wow! That is really cool!" said Robbie.

All of a sudden, Chloe started screaming, "A snake! A snake!"

"That is not a snake," said Jon. "That is an eel. They look like snakes, but they are fish."

"Are they poisonous, like some snakes?" asked Robbie.

"They can be," said Jon. "They hide in caves or holes in the coral and wait for their prey to swim by. Then they pop out and grab it in their sharp teeth."

Chloe covered her eyes. "I can't look at it," she said. "It's too scary. I am going to have nightmares!"

"What's that long, skinny fish?" I asked.

"That's a pipefish," said Jon.

"It's really weird-looking."

"I like that orange-and-white-striped one over there," said Jessie.

"That's called a clown fish," said Jon. "You probably remember that fish from the movie *Finding Nemo*."

"I love that movie!" said Jessie.

"Look at that pretty blue one over there," said

Chloe. "It matches the blue nail polish I put on today."

"All right, everybody," said Jon. "Follow me through the tunnel of fish. I have something to show you in the next room."

We walked through the tunnel, and the fish

were swimming all around us. They were even swimming over our heads.

"I feel like I'm scuba diving," I said to Robbie. "This is so cool. I can't wait to see what Jon's going to show us next!"

CHAPTER 4

Moon Jellies

"Walk right over here and look in this tank," Jon said.

"What are these?" asked Max. "They look like aliens."

"Moon jellies!" Robbie said.

"That's right," said Jon. "These are a kind of jellyfish called moon jellies."

"Wow!" we all said.

Chloe backed away from the tank. "I don't like jellyfish," she said. "They sting you."

"My cousin got stung by a jellyfish once," said Max. "He got this really bad rash all over his leg."

"Many jellyfish do sting," said Jon. "But not moon jellies."

Chloe moved a little closer.

"Their tentacles have some venom, but if one touched your leg, you probably wouldn't even feel the sting."

"Then how do they catch their prey?" Robbie asked.

"That bell-shaped part is their body. It's covered with this sticky stuff, and small animals like brine shrimp get stuck there."

"How do they eat it?" asked Jessie.

"They use their tentacles to move the food into their mouths."

"That's kind of weird," I said, laughing. "It's like if I was hungry at breakfast, I would swim around until a pancake got stuck to my head. Then I would pull it out of my hair and eat it."

We all started laughing.

"Yep, that's about right," said Jon.

"They look so squishy," said Max.

"That's because their bodies are ninety-five percent water," said Jon.

"But we have a lot of water in *our* bodies," said Robbie.

"But our bodies are not big blobs, because we have something very important that holds us up. Does anyone know what that is?" asked Jon.

"Our skeleton!" we all shouted.

"Yes!" said Jon. "Humans have a skeleton. But moon jellies do not have a skeleton inside their bodies, like us, or a hard outer shell, called an exoskeleton, like a lobster. So they are like big bowls of jiggly jelly."

"When they move, they look kind of like those bath toys that squirt water," said Max.

"Max Sellars has bath toys?" I said to Robbie.

"*You* play with toys in the bathtub?" Chloe said to Max.

Max's face turned red. "I-I-I didn't say I played with them," he stammered. "I just said they look like them."

"Well, they do squirt water," said Jon. "They take water into their bell, and then they squirt it out behind them to move forward."

"Next time I go to the beach, I'm going to look for a moon jelly," said Robbie.

"Me, too," I said.

"You probably won't see any," said Jon.

"Why not?" I asked.

"Because moon jellies live in tropical oceans. They like to swim in water that is warm."

"Me, too," said Chloe. "I will only go swimming in my nana's pool if it's eighty-five degrees."

"Eighty-five degrees!" said Robbie. "That's not a swimming pool. That's a hot tub!"

"Oh, she has one of those, too," said Chloe. "And—"

"Not now, Chloe," said Mrs. Wushy. "We are not talking about your nana's hot tub. You need to listen to Jon."

"There is something else about moon jellies that is very interesting," said Jon.

"I know," said Chloe. "They glow in the dark."

"Glow in the dark?" Jessie said to me. "Where does she come up with this stuff?"

"No, they don't glow in the dark," said Jon. "What I was going to say was that they have no brains and no blood."

"Hey, no brains . . . just like you, Chloe," Max said, laughing.

"Max Sellars, you take that back right now!" said Chloe, stamping her foot. "You are such a meanie!"

Max just kept laughing.

"Mrs. Wushy!" Chloe whined. "Max is being mean to me again. He said I have no brains."

"Max, that is not a nice thing to say," said Mrs. Wushy. "You need to tell Chloe you're sorry."

Max just stared at Mrs. Wushy.

"Now, Max."

"Yeah, now, Max," said Chloe, wagging her finger in Max's face.

"Sorry," Max mumbled.

"Please look at Chloe, and say it loud enough so she can hear you," said Mrs. Wushy.

"Sorry!" Max shouted in Chloe's face.

"Max," said Mrs. Wushy, "this is your last warning. Next time you will have to take a break with me and miss part of the tour."

"But . . ."

"No buts. Jon has a lot to show us today, but you two are wasting our time. Do you think you're ready to be a good listener?"

Max nodded.

"All right, then," said Jon. "I think it's time to go into the next room. Let's pretend to swim over there. Okay?"

Jon moved his hands in the air like he was swimming.

"Look at me!" said Jessie. "I'm doing the breaststroke."

"I'm doing the backstroke," said Max.

"Max," said Mrs. Wushy, "I don't think that's safe. You can't see where you are going. Please turn around."

Just as she said that, Max crashed into me. I went flying and hit the ground.

"Freddy, are you all right?" asked Mrs. Wushy.

"I'm fine," I said, slowly getting up off the floor.

Mrs. Wushy grabbed Max's hand. "You can walk with me," she said.

CHAPTER 5

Sea Turtles

As soon as we got into the next room, we all ran over to the big tank in the middle of it and pressed our noses against the side. "Oooooh, sea turtles!" said Jessie. "My favorite!"

"Look at how big they are!" I said.

"I wish I could go swimming with one," said Robbie.

"I wish I could take a ride on its back," I said. "That would be so much fun!"

"These are loggerhead sea turtles," said Jon.

"Does anyone want to guess why they are named that?"

Robbie, the science genius, raised his hand. "Because they have log-shaped heads," he said.

"Right!" said Jon.

"Why do they keep sticking their heads out of the water?" asked Jessie.

"Because they need to get air," said Jon. "They don't have gills like fish. They have lungs, like us, so they have to come up to the surface to breathe."

"But some of these guys have been under for a long time," I said.

"Loggerheads can stay underwater for up to thirty minutes at a time, and then they have to come up for air," said Jon.

"Wow! Thirty minutes!" said Jessie. "That's a long time. I wish humans could do that."

"I wish I could swim like them. They are pretty good swimmers," I said.

"That's because they have flippers instead of feet," said Jon.

"Hey, I have flippers!" said Max.

"Then you must be a mermaid," said Chloe.

"Is she still talking about mermaids?" Jessie asked, rolling her eyes.

"I'm not a mermaid!" Max said, and glared at Chloe. "I mean I wear flippers sometimes, when I go swimming in the pool."

"And why do you do that?" asked Jon.

"They make me go a lot faster. I almost

always win a swimming race if I have my flippers on," said Max, smiling.

"The flippers make these turtles move a lot faster, too," said Jon. "Did you know that because of their flippers, sea turtles can swim seventy-five miles in the same amount of time it takes a land turtle to walk just one mile?"

"No way!" we all said.

"That's amazing," said Mrs. Wushy.

"Do these turtles ever come out of the water?" asked Max.

"Yes, they do," said Jon.

"But how do they walk if they don't have feet?"

"It's hard for them to move around. That's why they don't come out of the water very often."

"Then why do they come out of the water at all?" asked Jessie.

"Well," said Jon, "the female turtles come up on the beach once a year, at night, to make their nests and lay their eggs."

"How do they make a nest?" I asked.

"They have claws on their front flippers that they use to dig a hole in the sand. After they dig the hole, one turtle can lay up to a hundred and twenty eggs at once. Then she buries them."

"A hundred and twenty eggs!" said Robbie. "That's ten dozen eggs!"

"So he's a science genius *and* a math genius," I thought.

"That's a lot of eggs," said Chloe.

"Yes, it is," said Jon. "But they have to lay a lot of eggs, because most of the baby sea turtles won't survive."

"What do you mean?" asked Robbie.

"Only one egg out of every three thousand will result in an adult sea turtle."

"Only one in three thousand!" said Jessie. "What happens to the rest of them?"

"Most of the eggs are eaten by other animals, like snakes, raccoons, and foxes, before they hatch."

"Aaaawwwww," we all said.

"How long does it take for them to hatch?" I asked.

"About two months. They hatch at night and then the turtles try to scurry down to the water before a predator attacks them."

"Can't their mom protect them?" asked Jessie.

"No. The mother sea turtle digs a hole, lays

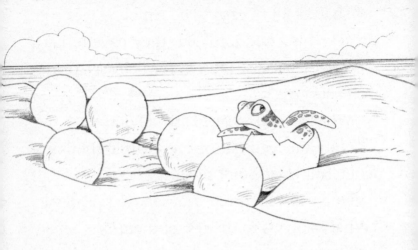

her eggs, covers them with sand, and then she goes back into the ocean."

"You mean she doesn't stay with the eggs?"

"No. That's why so many of them get eaten. There really isn't anything protecting them," said Jon.

"Those poor itty-bitty babies," said Chloe. "They must be so scared without their mommies."

"Once they hatch, they are on their own," said Jon.

"We learned about endangered animals," said Mrs. Wushy. "Are sea turtles endangered?"

"Yes, they are," said Jon.

"Why?" asked Jessie.

"There are a few reasons," Jon said. "Some people hunt the turtles for their shells. You can sell a turtle shell for a lot of money. Some turtles die by accident because they get caught up in huge fishing nets, like the ones used to catch tuna for people to eat. And some turtles are dying because their habitat is getting polluted."

"What do you mean?" I asked.

"Remember those moon jellies we saw in the other room?"

We nodded.

"Loggerhead turtles like to eat moon jellies, but to them, a floating plastic bag looks just like a moon jelly. If someone has a picnic on the beach and doesn't throw out their trash, then their sandwich bag can end up in the ocean. A loggerhead turtle can eat it by mistake, thinking it's a moon jelly. If the turtle does swallow the bag, it will die because it can't breathe."

"That's really sad," said Jessie.

"Yes, it is," said Jon. "That's why we all have to take care of planet Earth and protect all living creatures. Make sure you pick up all your trash."

"Don't be a litterbug," said Robbie, "because your trash could end up in the ocean."

"That's right!" said Jon. "Now, how would you all like to touch a real, live sea creature?"

"Really?" said Jessie.

"Can we?" asked Robbie.

"Right this way," said Jon.

CHAPTER 6

Wet 'n' Wild

Max pushed his way to the front of the line. "Do we really get to touch animals?" he asked Jon.

"Yes."

"Where? When?"

"Right here. Right now," said Jon.

He led us into a room that had a big touch tank. "Come over here, everybody, and find a place where you can reach into the water."

We all quickly found a spot and stuck our hands in the water. Everyone except Chloe.

"Come right over here," said Jon. "I've got a spot just for you."

"No, thank you," said Chloe. "I just got my fingernails painted, so I can't put them in water." She held her hands up in front of her face.

"Who is she kidding?" Jessie whispered. "She is just too afraid to touch something that's not pink and fluffy."

"She doesn't know what she's missing," said Robbie.

"These are all animals you would find in a tide pool," said Jon. "Feel free to touch them and pick them up. Just remember to be gentle."

"Look at this orange starfish," said Jessie.

"Scientists who study ocean animals are called marine biologists," said Jon. "These aren't named starfish, because they aren't fish. They're called sea stars. That one is a bat star."

"What is this?" asked Max, holding up something long and fat.

"That has a really funny name," said Jon. "It's called a sea cucumber."

"Ha, ha, ha," said Max. "It does look like a cucumber, but I wouldn't want to eat it. It feels kind of squishy."

"Eeeeewwwww!" said Chloe, taking two steps back.

"I found a hermit crab," I said. "But it looks like it has a snail shell."

"It does have a sea snail shell," said Jon. "Hermit crabs need a shell to protect themselves, but they don't have their own shells. They have to find shells that other sea creatures left behind. There are some sea snails in this tank. That hermit crab must have found an empty snail shell and crawled inside."

"That's kind of weird," I said, laughing. "It's like they are borrowing someone else's house."

"What's this prickly pink thing?" asked Jessie.

Chloe took a step closer. "Did you say 'pink'?"

"That's a sea urchin," said Jon. "You can touch it. It won't hurt you."

Chloe shook her head, but Jessie touched it. "This is so much fun!" said Jessie. "I could stay here all day."

"About one more minute, and then we have to move on, everybody," said Jon.

"AAAAAAWWWWWW!" we all moaned.

"I know you are having fun here, but I have another creature for you to touch."

After a minute, we followed Jon into the next room, where there was another touch tank with something big swimming around in it.

Max ran over and was about to reach his hand into the water when Jon stopped him. "Hold on there, buddy. I have some important rules to tell you before you stick your hands in there."

Chloe leaned over and looked in the tank. "What are those?" she asked, wrinkling up her nose. "They look like bats."

"Those are cownose rays," said Jon.

"You mean stingrays?" said Robbie. "We get to touch stingrays? I've never touched a stingray before!"

"Do they really sting?" asked Chloe.

"They can," said Jon.

Chloe started running around the room, screaming, "AAAAAAHHHHH!!! Get me out of here! Get me out of here!"

Mrs. Wushy grabbed her. "Chloe, why are you screaming? Calm down."

"That thing is going to sting me! That thing is going to sting me!" she wailed, pointing to the ray.

"No, it's not," said Mrs. Wushy. "Even though it has fins that look like wings, it can't fly out of the water."

"When you touch them," said Jon, "you use just two fingers and touch their wings only. Their stinger is on their tail, so if you stay away from the tail, you will be fine."

"Can we touch them now?" Robbie asked.

"Go right ahead," said Jon.

We all stuck our hands in the tank, except for Chloe. She ran to the other side of the room to hide in the corner.

"She's silly," said Jessie. "These rays are beautiful."

"I wish I could have one as a pet," I said.

"That would be so cool. I could keep it in the bathtub."

"Yeah, right. Your mom won't even let you have a dog!" Robbie said, laughing. "She would freak out if you brought one of these home!"

"Rays are cousins of sharks," said Jon. "They both have a skeleton made of . . ."

"Cartilage," I said, finishing Jon's sentence.

"Very good," said Jon.

"Sharks and rays don't have any bones in their bodies like other fish," I said. "Their skeleton is made of cartilage."

"What is cartilage?" asked Jessie.

"It's the hard stuff your fingernails are made of," I said.

"Someone knows a lot about sharks," said Jon. "We have a new shark exhibit here at the aquarium."

"I know," I said. "I can't wait to see it!"

"Freddy is a shark expert," said Jessie. "You

can ask him anything about sharks, and he knows the answer."

"Really?" said Jon. "Well, after lunch, we're going to go see the sharks, and I'll give you the shark quiz."

"Shark quiz?" said Jessie. "What's that?"

"It's ten questions about sharks. If you can answer all ten questions, then you win a prize. So far, none of the kids on my tours have been able to answer all ten questions," said Jon.

"Just wait until Freddy gets over there," said Jessie. "He'll be able to answer all ten questions, no problem. Right, Freddy?"

I gulped. "Right," I said.

"As long as I have my lucky shark's tooth," I thought.

CHAPTER 7

The Shark Quiz

After lunch, Jon took us to the shark exhibit.

"Wow!" I said. "This is amazing."

"Come over here, everybody," said Jon. "I want to show you something I bet you've never seen before."

"What are those?" asked Max.

"Those are shark eggs."

"Eggs?" said Chloe. "But they're not round. They're flat. Eggs are supposed to be round."

"Well," said Jon, "shark eggs are shaped like a rectangle, and they are flat."

"Do all sharks hatch from eggs?" asked Jessie.

"Good question," said Jon. "No, all sharks do not hatch from eggs. Some hatch from eggs, like birds. Some are born alive from their mothers, like human babies. And some hatch inside their mothers and then come out."

"That is very interesting," said Mrs. Wushy. "I never knew that."

"Now look around you," said Jon. "There are tanks with all kinds of sharks. Sharks come in all shapes and sizes."

I ran over to one tank and pressed my nose against the glass. I couldn't believe my eyes.

Jessie came and stood next to me. "What kind of shark is that?" she asked. "It's the same as the one on your shirt."

"It's a hammerhead shark," I said.

"It's pretty big," said Jessie.

"It sure is," I said. The hammerhead swam right past me. "I have never been this close to one before. This is so awesome!"

"Freddy, Freddy, come over here," said Robbie. "Tell me what kind of shark this is."

"It's a blacktip reef shark. See how it has black on the tips of its fins? Isn't it beautiful?"

Chloe interrupted us. "It's not beautiful," she said. "It's scary! I don't think I want to go swimming anymore."

"These sharks don't live in the oceans near us," I said. "You don't need to worry about seeing one of these guys when you go to the beach."

Max was peering into another tank. "This shark is funny-looking," he said. "It looks like it has whiskers."

I went over to where he was. "That's a nurse shark," I said. "They mostly stay on the ocean floor."

"Wow!" said Jon. "You really *do* know a lot about sharks! I'm impressed."

"Thanks!" I said, smiling.

"Why don't you give him that quiz?" asked Jessie. "I bet Freddy knows all of the answers."

"Some of the questions are kind of hard," said Jon. "Like I said, I still haven't met a student who can answer all of the questions correctly."

"Well, Freddy can do it," said Jessie. "Right, everybody?"

"Fred-dy! Fred-dy!" the whole class started chanting.

"Why doesn't everybody sit down here on the floor in the middle of the room? You can all watch the sharks swim around while I ask Freddy the questions."

Everyone sat down except me. "Come on over here, Freddy," said Jon. "Are you ready for question number one?"

I nodded and smiled.

"What is the biggest living shark?" asked Jon.

"This one is easy," I said. "The whale shark. They can be as big as sixty feet long."

"Right!" said Jon.

Jessie clapped her hands. "Good job, Freddy!"

"Question number two: What is the fastest shark?"

"The mako shark. Makos can swim up to twenty miles per hour."

"Right again," said Jon.

I smiled.

"Question number three: What are baby sharks called?"

"Pups!" This was going to be easier than I had thought!

"Question number four: Name one shark that eats plankton."

"The megamouth."

"Oooh," said Chloe. "That one sounds really scary."

"It's really very gentle," I said.

"Question number five," Jon said. "How many teeth can a shark have at one time?"

"About three thousand, I think."

Jon nodded.

"Way to go, Freddy!" said Jessie. "You're halfway done!"

I took a deep breath.

"Ready for the rest of the questions?" asked Jon.

I nodded.

"Question number six: What is the smallest shark?"

"The dwarf lantern shark. It is only about six inches long and weighs less than one pound."

"Are you really just six years old?" asked Jon.

"Yep," I said.

Jessie giggled.

"Question number seven: How long have sharks existed?"

"Over three hundred million years. They are older than the dinosaurs."

"Really?" said Max. "Cool!"

"Question number eight: What shark has the longest tail?"

"Easy peasy," I said. "The thresher shark. I know all about thresher sharks. Did you know that my last name is Thresher?"

"You really are a shark boy," said Jon, smiling.

"Only two questions left, Freddy," said Jessie.

"Question number nine: How much can a great white shark weigh?"

"I know this. I just saw a TV show about great whites the other night. It said they can weigh up to seven thousand pounds."

"Amazing," said Jon. "You're right again."

"Only one question left," said Robbie. "If you get it right, you win the prize!"

"Ready?" asked Jon.

"Ready," I said.

"Question number ten: What is the only shark that can live in both freshwater and salt water?"

"Ummmm . . . ummmm . . . ," I stammered.

"Uh-oh," said Jessie.

"I know this. I know this," I said to myself. I reached for my lucky shark's tooth to rub it. Rubbing it always brings me good luck. But when I reached for it, it wasn't there. "Oh no!" I shouted. "Oh no!"

Mrs. Wushy ran over. "Freddy, are you all right?"

"My lucky shark's tooth! It's gone! I can't finish without my lucky shark's tooth! I've got to find it!"

CHAPTER 8

Lost!

"Maybe it fell off in this room, and somebody is sitting on it," said Mrs. Wushy. "Let's have everybody stand up."

Mrs. Wushy is so smart. I was freaking out, and my shark's tooth was probably right there in the room.

"Would you all please stand up for a minute and look on the floor where you were sitting?"

The whole class stood up. I held my breath. Everybody looked around them on the floor.

"Does anybody see it?" asked Mrs. Wushy.

"No! Not me!"

"Not me!"

"I've got to find that shark's tooth," I said. "It's a special present from my papa and grammy, and it's my good-luck charm."

Jessie jumped up and down. "I'll help you, Freddy."

"I will, too," said Robbie.

"Me, too," said Max.

I blinked. I couldn't believe that Max Sellars was really going to help me with something, but right now I needed all the help I could get.

"Come on, guys!" I said. "Let's go!"

Jessie, Robbie, Max, and I all started running out of the room.

"Wait!" said Mrs. Wushy. "I don't want you running around the aquarium by yourselves. Jon will take you back to the rooms we were already in and help you look for it. The rest of us will stay here."

"When you lose something," said Jon, "the best thing to do is to retrace your steps."

"That's what my dad always says," I said.

"Sounds like this isn't the first time you've lost something," Jon said, smiling.

I looked at him. "I probably lose something once a week."

"But the good news is," said Robbie, "you always find it."

"We are going to find your shark's tooth, Freddy," said Jessie. "Don't worry!"

"We just *have* to find it," I said. "I can't go home without it!"

Jon took us to the very first room we had been in, with all the beautiful fish. "I wish they could talk," I said. "Then they could tell us if they see my tooth."

Max pretended to swim over to me. "Blub, blub, blubbie, blub," he said in my ear.

"What are you doing?" I said, trying to push him away. I knew it wasn't a good idea to have him come along.

"You said you wished the fish could talk. I'm a talking fish. Blub, blubbie, blub."

Jessie giggled.

I smiled a little.

"Made you smile!" said Max.

"Okay, let's all spread out to look for the tooth," I said.

We all went to different parts of the room, but we didn't find anything.

"I don't think it's in here," said Jon. "Let's move on."

We went to look in the room with the moon jellies. Nothing.

We didn't find it in the sea turtle room, either.

"We're never going to find it!" I said, trying to hold back my tears. I put my head in my hands. I really wanted to cry, but if I did, Max would call me a crybaby. I didn't know which was worse—losing the shark's tooth, or having Max call me a crybaby for the rest of my life!

"Come on, Freddy," Jessie said, grabbing my hand. "We still have one area left."

I walked slowly into the first touch-tank room.

Max picked up a sea star. "It's not under here!" he said, laughing.

How could he laugh at a time like this?

"If it fell in here, I hope one of these critters didn't eat it," said Jessie.

"Oh no! I never thought of that!" I said.

"Not to worry," said Jon. "They wouldn't eat it."

I wiped my forehead. "Phew!" I said.

We pushed around the little rocks that were on the bottom of the touch tank. "I don't see it," said Robbie.

The room seemed kind of quiet. I looked up from the touch tank. "Uh, where's Max?" I said.

Just then we all heard him yelling from the next room. "Come quick! Come quick!"

"I hope he's all right," said Jon. "This is why we all need to stick together!"

We ran into the room with the rays.

Max was holding something in his hand and jumping up and down. "Guess what I found?" he said.

"What?" I asked.

"Your shark's tooth!"

"You did?" I asked. "Where?"

"In the ray tank," said Max.

"You mean in the water?" I asked.

"Yep," Max said, smiling.

"I wonder how it got in there."

"It must have fallen off your pants when you leaned over to touch the rays," said Jessie.

"Here you go, Freddy," said Max, handing me the tooth.

"Thanks, Max," I said. "I owe you big-time."

"Yes, you do," Max said, grinning. "Yes, you do!"

I kissed the shark's tooth. "I'm so glad you're back," I said to it.

Jon laughed. "I think we should get back to the rest of the class."

We walked to the shark room.

"Did you find it, Freddy?" asked Mrs. Wushy.

"Actually, Max found it," I said.

"Really?" said Mrs. Wushy. "I am proud of you, Max, for being such a great helper."

"Now can Freddy finish the shark quiz?" asked Jessie.

"Do you want to, Freddy?" asked Jon.

"Yes, I do! I do! I do! I do!"

"Okay, then. You had one question left. Question number ten: What is the only shark that can live in both freshwater and salt water?"

I rubbed my shark's tooth for good luck. "It's

the bull shark. Bull sharks can live in the ocean and in freshwater."

"That's right!" said Jon.

The whole class cheered. "Hooray for Freddy! Hooray for Freddy!"

"You win the prize." Jon handed me a shark trophy with the words *Shark Expert* written across it.

"That is amazing," said Jon. "You are the first person to answer all ten questions. How did you know all the answers?"

"With a little brains and"—I patted my shark's tooth—"a little luck."

I grew up in California and spent a lot of time playing in the ocean. I would swim, jump in the waves, body board, and snorkel. I have amazing memories of my days at the beach.

The world's oceans provide us with oxygen, bring rain to farmlands, give us places to play, and are the homes of beautiful creatures. But the oceans are in trouble: Trash is floating on the waves, cargo ships are spitting out pollution, and innocent marine life is being scooped up by fishing nets.

If you love the oceans, and the things that live in them, then you can help. Learn all you can about the threats facing our oceans. Read books, such as *50 Ways to Save the Ocean* by David Helvarg, to discover what you can do to help. Most important, get involved and make your voice heard. Participate in a beach cleanup or start a Save the Oceans club at your school. One person can make a difference.

I hope you have as much fun reading *Shark Attack!* as I had writing it.

HAPPY READING!

Abby Klein

Freddy's Fun Pages

FREDDY'S SHARK JOURNAL

FREDDY'S FAVORITE SHARK FACTS

The largest living shark is the whale shark. It can be up to sixty feet long.

The smallest shark is the dwarf lantern shark. It is only six inches long.

There are between 375 and 475 species of sharks.

Sharks have existed for over 300 million years. They are older than the dinosaurs.

Most sharks live to be about twenty-five years old in the wild.

A great white shark can weigh up to seven thousand pounds!

The thresher shark has the longest tail.

The fastest shark is the mako shark. It can swim up to twenty miles per hour.

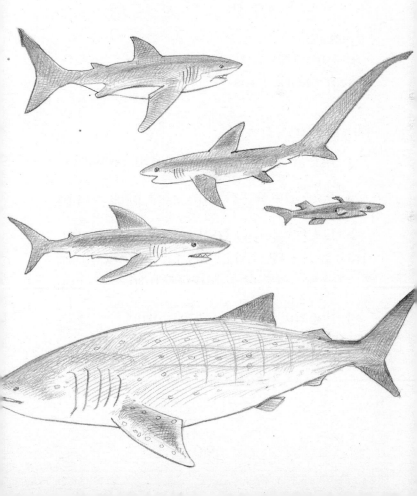

EDIBLE AQUARIUM

The next time you have a party, make these mini aquariums that you and your friends can eat!

YOU WILL NEED:

blue Jell-O
gummy fish
clear plastic cups

DIRECTIONS:

1. Ask an adult to help you make Jell-O.

2. Pour the Jell-O into clear plastic cups.

3. Let the Jell-O cool in the refrigerator until it is PARTIALLY set (about one hour). Then place a few gummy fish in each cup.

4. Put the Jell-O back into the refrigerator until it is completely set.

Eat and enjoy!

JELLYFISH DECORATION

Would you like to make a moon jelly like the ones Freddy and his friends saw at the aquarium?
Just follow these simple steps.

YOU WILL NEED:

a paper plate
markers or paints
colored tissue paper
scissors
tape

DIRECTIONS:

1. Cut the paper plate in half to make a semicircle. This will be your jellyfish's body.

2. Decorate half of the plate any way you like using markers or paint.

3. Cut strips of tissue paper about one inch wide and six inches long. These are your jellyfish's tentacles.

4. Tape one end of each strip of tissue paper to the back of the plate and let the rest of the strip hang down. Add as many tentacles as you wish.

5. You can use the other half of the plate to make a second jellyfish if you like!

SEA STAR NECKLACE

The kids got to touch sea stars at the aquarium. Make your own sea star to hang around your neck!

YOU WILL NEED:

white glue
waxed paper
sand or glitter
a paper clip
yarn

DIRECTIONS:

1. Lay out a piece of waxed paper.

2. Squeeze glue onto the waxed paper in the shape of a sea star. Make sure it has five arms! After you make the outline with glue, fill in the whole thing with glue as well.

3. Fold a paper clip into a V shape and put the ends of the paper clip into the glue at the tip of one arm of the sea star, like a hanger.

4. Sprinkle the glue with sand or glitter. Shake off any excess.

5. Let the glue dry completely. You will probably have to let it sit overnight.

6. When it is completely dry, carefully peel the waxed paper off the back of your sea star.

7. Cut a piece of yarn as long as you like and slip it through the paper clip to make the cord for your necklace. Tie the ends of the yarn together.

8. Hang your necklace around your neck and show it off to your friends!